Theodore's Rival

by Edward Ormondroyd

illustrated by John Larrecq

Parnassus Press Berkeley, California

COPYRIGHT © 1971 BY EDWARD ORMONDROYD FOR STORY
COPYRIGHT © 1971 BY JOHN LARRECQ FOR ILLUSTRATIONS
PUBLISHED BY PARNASSUS PRESS
LIBRARY OF CONGRESS CATALOG CARD NUMBER 76-156876
LITHOGRAPHED IN THE UNITED STATES OF AMERICA
ISBN 0-87466-001-7

for Joan

Lucy had a birthday party and invited her friends and her smudgy old bear, Theodore. She could hardly wait to begin opening her presents. The moment her last guest arrived she said, *"Please,* Mother, now can I?" Her mother said, "All right," and everyone crowded around to see.

First she unwrapped a beach hat. 'The very thing to prevent sunstroke,' Theodore thought.

Then came a necklace with lots of dangles. 'Just what she's always wanted,' Theodore said to himself.

'Aha!' he remarked when Lucy unwrapped a large inflatable sea monster. 'This is going to be our best birthday yet!'

Everyone said "Ooh!" and "Ah!" and Theodore beamed happily as Lucy went on opening her presents. She unwrapped a pair of pyjamas, and a jigsaw puzzle, and color crayons, and a tea set, and a Winnie-the-Pooh book.

'A book about *me*,' Theodore thought with a proud sigh when he saw the picture on the cover.

Then Lucy's mother brought out the cake and ice

cream, and everyone sang "Happy Birthday To You," and
Lucy blew out the candles on the first puff. Just as they
were about to begin on the refreshments, the doorbell rang.

It was the mailman. He delivered a large package that

Lucy's Uncle Benjamin had sent all the way from Upper Darby, Pennsylvania. The package was very well wrapped, and Lucy needed a lot of help opening it. But finally she got down to the last layer of tissue paper and tore it away.

Everyone said "Ooh!" as she pulled out the gift. It had black and white fur, and two ears, and shiny black eyes, and...

'Oh no!' Theodore said to himself in a shocked whisper. 'Not—not another—*bear*? It can't be! *I'm* the bear in this family!'

He was so overcome that he fell off his chair.

"Oh, I love it!" Lucy cried. She hugged the newcomer hard. "Look," she said, "he has a key in his back!" She wound up the key, and tinkling music began to play.

"Oooooh!" Lucy said. "Oh, thank you, Uncle Benjamin! You know what, everybody? I'm going to call *him* Benjamin, too."

They all sat down again to finish their ice cream and cake. Benjamin sat in Lucy's lap and played his tune over and over.

'Benjamin!' Theodore snorted to himself. 'That's a dumb name for a bear, if you ask me. Listen to that silly tune! I could bang the piano with my *nose* and make better music than that.'

When the party was over they all went outside to play. Theodore was left by himself on the floor with his legs in the air. He imagined Lucy taking Benjamin for a ride on the swing, or around the block on her tricycle.

'You call *that* a bear?' he thought bitterly. 'He's too clean for a bear. He doesn't even make bearish sounds.

Why should Lucy need another bear, anyway? *One* bear in a family is just the right number. Uncle Benjamin must be pretty dumb if he doesn't know that!'

Later in the afternoon Lucy ran in without Benjamin, and picked Theodore up. "Come on, Theodore!" she said. "We're going to the supermarket."

He began to feel better as she carried him out. He loved to go to the supermarket and walk up and down the aisles with Lucy, looking at all the things they could buy if they were rich. But as soon as they were outside, Lucy dropped him in the shopping cart. Then she skipped ahead, carrying Benjamin. Lucy's mother pulled the cart.

Theodore bumped along behind them all, upside down and full of very dark thoughts.

Henry, the dog who always hung around in front of the supermarket, said, 'Good afternoon, Theodore,' as they went by.

'There's nothing good about it!' Theodore snapped. 'Nothing good at all!'

Lucy's mother let her push a store shopping cart of her own because it was her birthday. She put Benjamin and Theodore side by side in the child's seat, and began to wheel them through the store.

'Oh my!' Benjamin murmured. 'This *is* exciting!'

Theodore scowled at the dill pickles and pretended not to hear. 'Exciting!' he sneered to himself. '*I* think it's a terrible bore.'

Suddenly Lucy remembered that she wanted her mother to buy some animal crackers. She let go of the cart and rushed away. The cart kept rolling on by itself. It coasted half-way down the aisle, swerved to the left, and bumped into the shelves.

Benjamin was not very firmly placed in the cart because Lucy had been careless when she put him in. Now he tumbled out feet over ears, and fell with a thump behind some large cereal boxes. A few startled notes of his tune tinkled out. Then all was quiet.

'Oh my,' Theodore thought, 'how sudden. Well, these little accidents will happen. A pity.' And he began to hum to himself.

When Lucy came back she looked all over for Benjamin. Tears began to roll down her cheeks.

'Oh, come now,' Theodore muttered uneasily. 'There's no need for that.'

Lucy's mother helped her look, but she couldn't find Benjamin either. She got a box of animal crackers to make

Lucy feel better. Lucy opened the box, but she was crying too hard by now to eat a single cracker.

'This is getting serious!' Theodore thought.

Lucy's mother said to the check-out clerk, "My little girl lost her new panda somewhere in the store. Will you please phone me at this number if someone finds it?"

Theodore was thunderstruck. 'Panda?' he said to himself, as Lucy put him in the shopping cart on top of the groceries. *'Panda?* Why, I thought—Wait! That means *I'm* still the bear in the family! Oh, how stupid I've been! *Something must be done!'*

When they came out of the store, Lucy's mother stopped to look at the newspapers in the rack. Theodore nudged an animal cracker out of the cart for Henry.

'I'm sorry I snapped at you when we went in,' he said.

'Oh well, we all have our ups and downs,' Henry said.

'I wonder if you could give me a little assistance,' Theodore said. He nudged another animal cracker out of the cart. 'Just take me back into the store for a moment, will you? I seem to have left a friend behind.'

Lucy looked up just in time to see her bear being carried by the ear into the store. She screamed "Theodore!" and set out in pursuit.

Several store clerks cried, "Get out of here! Scoot! No dogs allowed!" They began to chase Henry.

'Where is your friend, by the way?' Henry mumbled through Theodore's fur.

'Just down this aisle, if you please,' said Theodore.

'No, sorry—I mean the next one.

'Oh dear, this isn't the one, either,' said Theodore.

'You'd better remember soon,' Henry panted. 'I'm going to be caught in a minute.'

'*Next* aisle!' Theodore said. 'I remember now!'

But clerks were closing in on them from both ends of the aisle. They were trapped.

'Over the top!' Theodore said. 'Jump!'

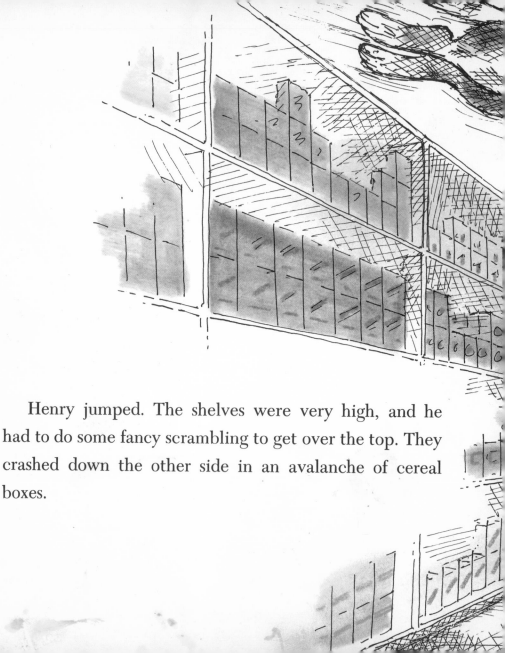

Henry jumped. The shelves were very high, and he had to do some fancy scrambling to get over the top. They crashed down the other side in an avalanche of cereal boxes.

'Ah, there,' said Benjamin. 'I was beginning to get worried.'

"Theodore!" Lucy cried. "And Benjamin!"

"I don't know what's gotten into Henry," said one of the clerks. "He never did anything like this before."

"But look—he found Benjamin!" Lucy said. "And I bet smart old Theodore showed him where to go!" She hugged all three of them as tightly as she could.

'She may be careless at times,' Theodore explained to his new friend, 'but she *does* understand bears! And pandas too, of course.'

Lucy insisted on taking Henry home so she could reward him. She gave another party, with animal crackers and left-over ice cream. Benjamin played his tune over and over. Henry ate all the animal crackers in two gulps while Lucy was looking the other way. And Theodore, with new chocolate smudges in his fur, beamed at everyone and thought, 'There can't be many families in the world that have a panda as tuneful as Benjamin *and* a bear as smart and resourceful as ME.'